To Kathryn Cole,
who keeps the sky from falling.
– W.Z.

One day Henny Penny
was eating corn in the farmyard
when . . .

whack! . . . an acorn fell on her head.

"Oh, my," said Henny Penny.
"The sky is falling! The sky is falling.
I must go and tell the King."

So she went along and she went along and she went along until she met Cocky Locky.

"Hello, Henny Penny," said Cocky Locky.
"Where are you going?"

"The sky is falling and I must go
and tell the King," said Henny Penny.

"Oh! May I go with you?"
asked Cocky Locky.

"Certainly!" said Henny Penny.

So they went along and they went along
and they went along until they met
Ducky Lucky.

"Hello, Henny Penny and
Cocky Locky," said Ducky Lucky.
"Where are you going?"

"The sky is falling and
we must go and tell the King,"
said Henny Penny and Cocky Locky.

"Oh! May I go with you?"
asked Ducky Lucky.

"Certainly!" said Henny Penny
and Cocky Locky.

So they went along and they went along
and they went along until they met
Goosey Loosey.

"Hello, Henny Penny, Cocky Locky and
Ducky Lucky," said Goosey Loosey.
"Where are you going?"

"The sky is falling and we must go and tell the King," said Henny Penny, Cocky Locky and Ducky Lucky.

"Oh! May I go with you?" asked Goosey Loosey.

"Certainly!" said Henny Penny, Cocky Locky and Ducky Lucky.

So they went along and they went along
and they went along until they met
Turkey Lurkey.

"Hello, Henny Penny, Cocky Locky,
Ducky Lucky and Goosey Loosey," said
Turkey Lurkey. "Where are you going?"

"The sky is falling and we must
go and tell the King," said Henny
Penny, Cocky Locky, Ducky Lucky
and Goosey Loosey.

"Oh! May I go with you?" asked
Turkey Lurkey.

"Certainly!" said Henny Penny,
Cocky Locky, Ducky Lucky and
Goosey Loosey.

So they went along
and they went along

and they went along
until they met Foxy Loxy.

"Greetings, Henny Penny, Cocky Locky, Ducky Lucky, Goosey Loosey and Turkey Lurkey," said Foxy Loxy. "Where are you going?"

"The sky is falling and we must go and tell the King," said Henny Penny, Cocky Locky, Ducky Lucky, Goosey Loosey and Turkey Lurkey.

"You'll never get there in time," said Foxy Loxy. "Come with me and I'll show you the shortcut."

"Certainly!" said Henny Penny,
Cocky Locky, Ducky Lucky,
Goosey Loosey and Turkey Lurkey.
And they followed Foxy Loxy
right into his cave.

Henny Penny, Cocky Locky,
Ducky Lucky, Goosey Loosey and
Turkey Lurkey were never seen again . . .

. . . and no one ever told the King
the sky was falling.